Fully Charged

NICOLE PARKER &
Unfortunate Reads

Book Cover Art by Kit Fox Art
Independently Published by Unfortunate Productions LLC
ISBN: 979-8-9913742-0-0

Blurb

Jewel is a newly single mom who just wants to unwind in her rare time alone. The kids are away, and it's time for mama to play...with herself.

Except the off-brand batteries in her favorite tool die mid-session. When she replaces them with the industry leader, Ohm-azing, Jewel gets more than long lasting pleasure.

Wattson has been sent from Ohm-azing headquarters to ensure Jewel is 100% satisfied.

Fully Charged is a parody sentient object romance intended for audiences over 18 years old. This contains intimate relations between a human woman and a mythical pink rabbit. Read at your own risk!

Dedication

If you think you are ready for this, you aren't.

Content Considerations

The following sentient object romance story is a work of fiction and is classified as parody. If you saw the cover of this book and still picked it up, you should know it's about to get real weird, but we're going to warn you anyway.

This story contains intimate relations between a female human and a giant male pink rabbit. There are references to divorce (off page), children (female main character is a divorcée and her children are away with family during the story, but make an appearance in the epilogue), alcohol, drug use (off page), book harm (explicit), masturbation (female), p0rn use (off page), use of s*x toys (a *lot* of them), s*x toy malfunction, 0rgasm denial, a giant pink bunny, his drum, dad shoes, flavored j*zz, female €jaculation, 0ral s*x, penetrative s*x, mutual play with an absurd amount of unusual phallic toys, extremely nerdy electrical puns, dirty talk, TPS reports, and of course–batteries.

Contents

Chapter 1
Backpfeifengesicht

Jewel

I rarely get "me time" anymore, but today the house is blessedly quiet. My sister offered to take the kids this weekend for a sleepover with her brood, and it's the first time in four months I've had the house all to myself. I tried not to act too eager when she offered, but who am I kidding? I practically shoved those menaces out the door, whether they were ready or not. I love them to death, but mama needs a break.

Once the kids left, my mind started to race with all of the chores that needed doing. The dishes in the stainless steel kitchen sink are piled higher than should be humanly possible. The bathrooms haven't been deep cleaned in a hot minute. Maybe I could kill two birds with one stone and clean the tile while I take a bath? That's when it hit me that I really needed some self care. Cleaning while trying to relax? Good gravy.

So now, I'm sitting here on the couch sipping my second glass of wine, feeling loose and relaxed. The romance novel I've had hidden away from nosy nellies in my closet is just getting to the spicy part, and that familiar ache builds between my legs. What is it about a big blue alien that just gets you going? Besides the huge cocks and special features, of course. Ok, fine. It's probably the huge cocks and special features.

Suddenly, my chest warms with a flush. Is that from the book or the wine? It doesn't matter either way, really. Like I said, I never get time to myself, and it isn't like I've gotten any action in the four months since my divorce was finalized. If I'm being honest with myself, I got more action from my trusty rabbit vibrator than that shell of a man, anyway.

Thinking about my toy makes me perk up with interest. I'm alone, I'm tipsy, and I'm horny. The trifecta situation to have a little–or a long–session with my B.O.B.

Folding the corner of the page in my book to mark my place before shutting it, I set it on the coffee table as I rise from the couch. Looking down at the wine on the table, I squint my eyes as I come to a decision.

"Oh ho, you are coming with me, my friend." Giggling a little, I add, "Well, maybe you won't be *coming*, but I am certainly going to."

Swift steps carry me to the master bedroom. The room is a mess, the whole house really. Clean laundry sits unfolded in baskets near the armchair. The chair is also covered in clothes from the chaos of trying on outfits every morning, only to hate the way I look and proceeding to go through five options before I settle on one.

Everyone has one of those chairs, right? Is there a name for that chair? I feel like there should be a name for it like, *backpfeifengesicht,* which is what Germans call a particularly annoying person you want to slap in the face.

"I can think of a backpfurg... backfefe... baftach... ugh, whatever!" Clearly, I'm unable to actually pronounce the fanciful word, but that's not the point.

Dragging myself out of my squirrel-moment, I remember why I came back into the bedroom in the first place. Orgasms. Big, loud, *multiple* orgasms. It's bunny time!

Finishing the rest of my wine in two big gulps, I set the glass down on the nightstand before opening the drawer and reaching my hand to the very back to feel around for my snatch-blaster. It's buried in the deep recesses of the drawer so prying little eyes don't see it when they inevitably sneak in here to snoop around. They always say they didn't, but nine-year-olds aren't exactly that stealthy. Once, they tried to convince me a stray dog had broken into the house and eaten all the chocolate pudding from the fridge, going so far as to make fake pudding paw prints on the linoleum of the kitchen floor. A scoff escapes me as the memory replays while my hand pats around in the dark.

"Aha! There you are!" I squeal as my fingers feel the familiar satiny silicone of my Jackrabbit 5000. The thing is glorious. Hot pink with a curved shaft and bulbous head, its prized feature is the little rabbit-shaped appendage whose floppy ears vibrate at 5000 rpm around my clit. Wetness seeps from my core as I think about how much uninterrupted time we have together tonight. Well, the wine and the steamy alien book probably played a part, and now my utilitarian cotton panties are soaked straight through the gusset.

"Just you and me tonight, baby," I coo at the sweet pink rabbit in my hands, stroking it reverently. Stripping naked in a flash, the bed dips as my weight sprawls across the middle. Screw hiding under the sheets, there isn't anyone else in the house. Clearly I'm in the mood if the wetness dripping down my thighs is any indication, and the promise of overpowering climaxes has ramped it up another notch.

Lying back on the soft pillows and spreading my thighs, a shiver of anticipation runs up my body when my wet folds meet the cool air. It's time for mama to take herself to Pound Town.

Pressing the button once for steady, low vibration, I click the vibrator on and lay back. Starting with my breasts, I drag the vibrator down my body, pausing once at each nipple before heading south. The closer the toy gets to my cave of wonders, the wetter I get. Even though I should tease myself more, impatience wins out. There will be more time for that later, anyway. Right now, I want to get to the main attraction.

As soon as the tip of the rabbit touches my clit, my back bows off the bed and a loud moan escapes my lips. Reminding myself I can be as loud as I want, I press the vibe even harder to my love button until I am about to come. Removing the toy to hold off the orgasm, I drift it lower, circling my entrance before plunging it inside me. No need for more foreplay. My pussy may as well be Niagara Falls. It's so wet.

The vibrations are glorious, but I'm greedy. Clicking the button twice more, the vibrator amps up its speed and starts rotating inside me. The rabbit ears rest on either side of my clit and I know it isn't going to take long until I fall over the edge. A huge orgasm is building in my core, my hips bucking against my hand holding the toy.

"Oh fuck yes, come on!" I yell out to no one, ready to explode.

Suddenly, the toy stops buzzing.

"*No no no no no!* What happened?" Upset at my climax being interrupted, I click furiously on the toy's power button, to no avail. Just my luck, the batteries must have died. Unceremoniously removing the toy from my velvet lounge results in a loud squelching noise that echoes through the dark room. I can't be bothered to be grossed out right now. I have to fix this.

Frantically pushing open the battery compartment, anger floods me as I see the generic blue batteries inside. My ex-husband was always a skimpy bastard, and that must have applied to batteries, too. I never would have put off-brand batteries in something so important.

"I can't believe that asshole is *still* ruining my orgasms even though he isn't here!" Grumbling to myself, my butt-naked ass runs to the kitchen junk drawer to look for new ones. Nope, only shitty "Enerboom" batteries here too. Desperate, each of the TV remotes gets turned over and opened as I search for Ohm-azing batteries I can borrow from any unused device.

"Aha!" Four remotes and two kids' toys later, I have enough of the tried-and-true brand batteries to finish tonight's session, before I have to go to the store to get more. Hustling back to the bedroom, the batteries are swapped into the toy lightning quick. Greedily clicking the power button far too many times, the toy starts to vibrate and rotate at speeds that cannot be safe. Shrieking, I drop the toy on the bed, watching in horror as it spins out of control. *Is this thing about to explode?!*

Enthralled by the intensity of it all, it takes me a moment to realize the air around the Jackrabbit 5000 is starting to glow. The light emitting from the toy gets brighter and brighter, until a few seconds later, it culminates in a bright white flash that temporarily blinds me. When I try to open my eyes, it takes a while for them to adjust, but I do register that the violent buzzing has stopped. Finally, my eyes come into focus, but they don't land on my trusty pink toy. Instead, there is a gi-ant...pink... bunny? Shaking my head doesn't make the pink fever dream in front of me go away, and when my brain finally comes back online, I scream.

"What the fuck are you?!"

Chapter 2
A 100% Satisfaction Guarantee

Wattson

"**L**ooks like you already started without me, but it's no problem. This bunny can keep the party going and going and going. All. Night. Long."

Her eyes go wide and I take her in. The woman in front of me-and she is *all* woman– looks to be in her late thirties. Though, I have to admit I am not great at guessing these things. The expanse of bare skin filling my vision nearly makes my mouth water. This is no fine-boned bird of a woman. No, the hottie in front of me is soft in all the right places, but sturdy enough to take a pounding. Thick thighs snag my attention and I can't help but imagine gripping them while she rides me. Maybe even smacking that lucious ass and watching it jiggle while I rail her from behind. Sensing my perusal, she glances around the room and grabs a pillow, attempting to cover herself up.

"I said, what the fuck are you?" The quiver in her voice belies her nervousness, though she puts on a brave face.

I hop over to her. "Isn't that obvious, little carrot?" Grabbing the pillow from her hand, a spark of electricity passes between us with the contact. The voluptuous woman jerks her hand back, eyes wide. "I'm your new and improved B.O.B. Buzzy Orgasm Bunny."

"My buzzy orgasm bunny?" She whispers, dazed. My little carrot must be so overcome with excitement that she can't form her own thoughts. No worries, I can think for the both of us tonight.

Tossing the pillow to the side, I reach a paw out to her. As she places her hand in it, another jolt of titillating power passes between us, pulling her out of her shock.

"You're not real."

Shifting my gaze, I peer down at my fluffy pink fur before giving her a sly grin that says, *yep, seems pretty real to me.* She takes a seat on the bed, dropping her head in her hands.

"It's finally happening. I've hit my breaking point. The divorce. The kids. Now this." She gestures in my direction and gives a manic little laugh. "I'm chatting with my hallucinations."

"I'm as real as the G spot, babe," I say with a wink. "Just because it took a while to find me doesn't mean I don't exist." Hopping over to her, my big bunny body pushes her legs open gently so I can stand between them. "How about we pick up where you left off and I can show you exactly how real I am?"

"How about you back the fuck up and give me a moment to get a handle on this?"

"The only thing that's getting handled tonight is you." I wink and she glares back. You'd think someone who was on the verge of orgasming only moments ago would be more on board with this. "Didn't you feel that spark between us? Don't you want to feel more?"

"What I *want* is to understand how my vibrator is suddenly walking and talking." Ah, my little carrot is still confused about why I'm here. That's a problem that can be solved in a flash.

"Ohm-azing has a 100% satisfaction guarantee. Our systems could sense how unsatisfied our competitors left you, and we want to do whatever it takes to fix that. I can *personally* guarantee you'll be satisfied tonight."

She huffs out an incredulous laugh. "I'm perfectly capable of taking care of myself, thank you very much."

I've got more than enough power to deal with a little resistance. "But tonight, you don't need to. You're always taking care of others, little carrot. Tonight, let me take care of you. Let me help you forget your worries and make your fantasies come true." She glances away. "Let me make you feel good." Her arms cross as I continue. "Listen. You still seem a bit shocked. I get it, I've got that effect on people. But there's got to be something I can do." I give her my biggest, most pathetic, innocent look, using every ounce of bunny cuteness I have.

Her eyes roll back so far I'm surprised they don't get stuck in her head. "That look isn't going to work on me. I told you, I don't need any help rubbin' my nubbin. What I need help with is all the other shit in my life." She gestures towards a chair covered in clothes.

In a flash, I hop over and ZIP! BANG! POW! The laundry is folded and sorted into neat piles, then I place them in a basket of what appears to be some other clean clothes.

"Holy shit. That was fast," she mutters under her breath.

"Don't worry, little carrot, I know how to go slow when I need to." She fights to hold back a smile, and a smug grin lifts the edges of my lips. I'm making progress. "Now, tell me what else you need, beautiful."

"I'm not going to have you do chores all night. Thanks for the laundry, but why don't you just go back to Ohm-azing home base and call it a night?"

"Oh, I don't think you're 100% satisfied just yet. I'll find something myself." Hopping around the room, I look for something else to do.

"Thanks, really... I just... That's not what I want, seriously. Besides, it seems like a waste of your unique skills."

"Well, I am a personal massager. Why not let me work out some of that tension?" My innuendo is met with a narrow-eyed glare. "We can start with your shoulders and neck. See where it goes." Hopping onto the bed to crawl behind her, my paws tentatively land on her shoulders. When she doesn't immediately protest, I begin to knead her tense muscles like a contented kitten.

"So tight, little carrot." Working out the knots in her muscles causes her to groan. She starts to relax as I rub her shoulders and neck. "Let me do what I came here for. Let this bunny burrow."

Chapter 3

I Deserve Compensation

Jewel

I should stop this madness right now. I know that. I shouldn't be letting what is likely a mental-break induced apparition massage my shoulders. I shouldn't be leaning into his touch, closing my eyes, and letting out soft moans and grunts when he hits the right spots. And I should most definitely not be getting butterflies in my stomach when he calls me 'little carrot,' because what kind of nickname is that?

But this is the most pampered I've been in years. He folded the laundry for me, he's massaging my stiff neck and shoulders, and knowing he wants me completely satisfied has me ignoring all the things I shouldn't be doing. A niggling voice at the edge of my mind is trying to tell me it's incredibly pathetic that my bar for being taken care of is so low, but I shove away the errant thought and focus on the soft, but strong paws gliding over my back.

"That's it, little carrot. Just relax for me. Your only job right now is to keep making those pretty little noises of pleasure." His face comes to burrow in the crook of my neck, the impossibly fast wiggles of his nose on my skin causing me to let out another moan. The rapid movement almost feels like a mini-vibrator, which reminds me that my epic orgasm was so rudely interrupt-ed just a few minutes ago.

"Mmm, if you came here from Ohm-azing to make sure I'm satisfied, how are you going to do that?" My voice is breathy as I continue, while the big pink bunny never stops his ministra-tions. "Do you have... ungh... fresh batteries or something? Ah, yeah, right there."

I swear he chuckles against my skin. "Is this not satisfying, little carrot?"

"Well, it is," I hedge, "but shouldn't I be compensated some-how for the unfinished, um, *peak* I experienced due to the crap-py batteries?"

"Were you climbing a mountain, little carrot?" he purrs. "You can say it. *Orgasm*. Climax. Use that sweet little mouth to tell me you want to come."

My core clenches at the thought of this giant rabbit making me come. The way he talks makes me think he would absolutely rock my world.

What the fuck am I thinking?

Wrenching my body away from the bunny's mind-blowing paws, I launch myself to the wall opposite my bed, pressing my back against it so hard it's like I'm trying to phase through it.

He can't be real, right? Never taking my eyes off of Pepto Bismol Peter Cottontail, my fingertips pinch the thin skin of my forearm.

"Ouch!" *Ok then, I'm not asleep.*

"No, beautiful, you are most definitely not asleep." His statement makes me realize I must have unintentionally said that last part out loud. Even as my eyes widen, the bunny begins to stalk towards me. His movement is smooth, like a jungle cat on the prowl. The logical action would be to run, but instead I find myself fascinated by him. As he moves towards me, his ears slowly scissor back and forth, giving him a deceptively playful look. His slow approach makes me think he *wants* me to peruse his body.

Rolling my gaze from his fuzzy ears down his form, I realize he isn't actually all pink. Starting just under his inexplicably impressive muzzle is a swath of white fur that encompasses his stomach. His coloring is kind of like if a penguin was recovering from a harsh sunburn it got a week prior. On either side of his rounded belly sit two huge feet. I barely catch my laughter as I see his shoe of choice is a pair of royal blue flip flops. Is he a middle-aged dad?

Well, I guess dad bods *are* in right now. I certainly wouldn't mind snuggling up to that plush body. The fur is probably as unbearably soft everywhere as it was on his paws. While I've been frozen in place, the sneaky rabbit has closed the distance between us and is now nearly pressed against me. He stops just shy of actually touching me though, his fur a hair's breadth away from my skin.

"Oh, little carrot, I can smell how wet you are for me." His breath is warm against my lips, barely there but still not making contact. "Let me take care of that need for you. I won't stop until you're screaming my name, and even then I'll keep going and going and going."

My breathing is heavy, but somehow I manage to eke out, "What *is* your name?"

"Ahh, I was wondering when you'd ask what you'd be yelling all night. It's Wattson. And you are?"

My response is barely a whisper. "Jewel."

The dark chuckle he looses sends shivers of arousal straight to my already drenched pussy. "Well, Jewel, why don't you let me show you what a man with real power can do?"

Fuck. I think I'm gonna let this rabbit fuck me.

Chapter 4
It Pays To Do Laundry
Wattson

J ewel slowly nods her head, and that's all the go-ahead this bunny needs to really amp things up.

"Oh little carrot, the things I am going to do to you. I'll satisfy you until you can't take any more."

I make initial contact, licking and sucking down her neck, past her collarbone and down to her breasts. My plan is to focus more of my energy here, but when she moans my name, I lose control. Electric need has me dropping to the ground to throw one of her legs over my shoulder, opening her up for me. Her pussy is glistening with her arousal, clearly ready. Nuzzling my bunny nose against her soft heat, I prep her for what's about to come. Savoring the moment, I begin with gentle licks.

"Fuck, little carrot. You taste better than ripe dandelions on a perfect spring day." Continuing to lap at her hot box, I can see that she needs more when her body bucks against my tongue. Regretfully, I leave the entrance to her sugar cave, dragging my tongue through her dripping canyon, up to the peak of her pleasure. I give a long, hard suck on her clit. Immediately, she grinds on my face and grabs one of my ears, giving it a rough tug. That takes my dick from a AAA straight to a D, forcing a groan from my mouth.

"If you keep that up, little carrot, I'm not going to be able to keep my focus on you." She laughs, but begins stroking my ear from base to tip.

"More Wattson, I need more," she moans out, panting.

My whiskers tickle her cunt as I chuckle, but then I give her exactly what she wants. Rapidly thrusting my tongue deep inside her, my nose rubs against her clit. My nostrils twitch as I increase my nose vibration speed to surpass the power of her Jackrabbit 5000.

"Fuck!" she screams out, but I don't think about relenting. I keep tongue fucking her pussy, darting in and out as I find the perfect spot to nestle my buzzing nose. She reaches down and strokes both of my ears in tandem. I nearly become her own personal cream machine from the stimulation and pull back, ready to ask her to slow down, but she screams, "Don't you fucking stop, bunny boy! I was guaranteed satisfaction, and I'm getting it."

I grab onto her hips, like my life depends on it, focusing on lasting longer than her. Nothing outlasts Ohm-azing! This certainly shouldn't be any different. Determined, I build her back up, buzzing and tongue fucking her until her pussy clenches around me, and even then I continue my onslaught through her release. She gets her revenge, stroking my ears until I cannot stand it and unload my charge, exploding all over her floor.

Once she comes down from her orgasm, I kiss gently down the side of her leg, helping her place her foot back down on the ground. She looks at the mess I made in horror.

"Shit. Is that battery acid?"

I glance down at my cock, a drop of cum remaining at the tip of my positive terminal. Meeting her eyes, I wipe it up with my paw, extending it up towards Jewel with a grin.

"Don't be shy, little carrot. Why don't you try some and find out?"

Her eyes widen, but she grabs hold of my forearm and bends down, enveloping me with her soft lips and licking my discharge off the pads of my paw. I feel her tongue swirl around and suddenly I have several other ideas for her pretty mouth. She makes a face.

"Definitely not battery acid. More like one of those cotton candy energy drinks." She starts to fidget. "Well, I'm, um, satisfied. Thanks?"

"Oh, little carrot, we're just getting started. Remember, Ohm-azing has a 100% satisfaction guarantee. We won't finish until you're filled with siemens and you've come so hard you don't remember your name."

I hop up to stand, my energetic movement surprising her a bit. Using the opportunity of her stunned state to my advantage, I grip her hips and drag her over to the now empty laundry chair. I knew finishing the laundry would pay off!

A swift tug pulls her into my lap, her back to my chest, my legs spreading hers wide. With one of my paws, I focus on her tits, pinching an erect nipple, which I sorely neglected earlier. The other paw wraps around her waist, snaking between her full hips to find her slick clit.

As I start rubbing slow circles, I feel her ass grind against my cock.

"Little carrot, feel what you do to me. You should see how hot you look, completely on display." I kiss her neck. "When was the last time you took the time to fully appreciate this amazing body?"

"Wattson," she moans.

"I love hearing you say my name. I'll love it more when you're screaming it." I scrape my teeth along her sensitive skin, delighting when I feel her shudder. "Are you going to come for me again, little carrot?" Her response is a jumbled mess of sounds, letting me know she's close. I keep doing what I'm doing, bringing her closer to release. I could watch this woman fall apart all night. Thanks to the power of Ohm-azing, I just might.

Chapter 5

I'm Sorry, Did You Just Say Rotate?

Jewel

Fuck, I think I'm going to come again. I thought consecutive multiple orgasms were a myth or just some trait I wasn't blessed with, but this brilliant bunny bouncing me on his lap may very well prove me wrong.

Whatever he's doing to my clit feels electric - or is that my whole body that's buzzing? After I licked his not-battery-acid-cum off his paws, my tongue tingled like I had just licked a nine volt battery to test it, and a jolt ran through my body. Initially, I assumed it was just the aftershock of an epic orgasm, but now it feels a little like I snorted a double dose of pre-workout powder without going to the gym. My heart is beating rapidly, and I feel like I could ride this bunny's blaster for days. Hell, I almost think I could outlast Wattson, even if he is powered by Ohm-azing.

A frustrated moan tears from my lips because I'm so damn close to my second O, but I need more. I beg. "More, Wattson, fuck me!" Instead of using that trouser snake I've been dry-humping to fill my needy pussy, he pulls back.

Is it still called a trouser snake if he doesn't wear pants? What-ever, it doesn't matter. Where the fuck is he going!? Reaching for him only causes him to chuckle darkly.

"Does your sweet sleeve need to be stuffed, little carrot?" All I can do is nod and whine in response. "Well then, why don't you take your pick?"

Confusion stops the desperate grinding I was doing right before something moves under my ass. With a yelp, I scramble off his lap, barely catching myself before I land ass-first on the floor. His cock, if you can call it that, looks more like a sex toy than anything else. It's long, thick, and hot pink, with no discernible head. The surface looks smooth, but just before I can touch it to find out, it shrinks.

No, it isn't shrinking. He's... retracting his fucking cock? I'd say I can't believe what I'm seeing, but the Ohm-azing rabbit just made me come so hard I saw stars, so anything is possible.

A soft whirring sound accompanies the retreat of his literal *pocket* rocket, and just as I think it's gone for good, a new accessory emerges. This one is a soft teal color and looks like my Jackrabbit 5000 if it was on steroids.

"What the fuck?" Real sophisticated, I know, but it gets the point across. Pointing at the now retracting teal member, I question, "Can you morph your dick?!"

"Ah no, little one, I have a variety of pleasure poles I can rotate through to maximize your enjoyment." As he speaks, a bright orange double dragon dong takes the place of the teal toy. "Should I keep going? Or do you have a preference which cock I destroy you with tonight?" The orange monster retracts, a wand with purple glittery vibrating anal beads taking its place.

"I'm sorry, did you just say *rotate*? Like, a six-disc CD changer, but for cock?"

"More like a ten-disc changer, if you want to look at it that way," Wattson responds smugly.

"Ohhh fancy. We could never afford the ten-disc one for our ca– oh my God! Why do I keep getting distracted? My mind feels like it's going a mile a minute!" I can't think straight, and now I have all but lost that second climax I was about to reach.

"I know what you need, little carrot." A vibrator with a massive shaft clicks into place. It's hot pink at the tip, but along the shaft its clear surface shows lots of metal beads inside. A smaller appendage branches off from the base of his shaft, topped with what I think is a clit sucker. Before I can get a good look at it, Wattson yanks me back into his lap. "You think about too much all the time. Now, you're going to be a good girl, and let me do all the thinking for you."

Before I can protest, Wattson lifts my hips and I feel that soft silicone tip at my entrance. A little roll of my hips lets him know I'm ready, so he eases it in, one excruciating inch at a time. I want to move, but he's got me pinned in place with his paws on my hips, forcing me to go at his pace. When he bottoms out inside me, he stills again.

"Please! I need-oh!"

My plea is cut off when his entire shaft begins to vibrate. Wattson gives me no time to adjust, instead thrusting in and out of me at a punishing pace while he holds me steady above him. The orgasm I thought I lost comes barreling into me like a lightning strike, and I come on a cry.

"Oh little carrot, that was close, but it still wasn't my name. I suppose I'll have to try harder." He's still pounding me relentlessly when suddenly I feel those beads inside me start to rotate. They drag along my inner walls each time he impales me, the entire thing kicking up a notch in its vibration level.

"Fuck! Oh, ah! Mmph. Energize me, Daddy!"

My entire vocabulary seems to have devolved into curse words and nonsensical moaning. When Wattson slams me down onto his robocock this time, he holds me there, the shaft still vibrating and spinning. He sets that suction tip on my swollen clit, and I'm lost. Slamming my eyes closed, I swear I see Allesandro Volta instead of God when the most electrifying orgasm sweeps through me.

"Ohm My God! Wattson!"

"Ahh now that's better, little carrot."

Chapter 6

Break Out the Big Guns

Wattson

"You think you've got another one in you? Or is your battery completely drained?"

Jewel blinks slowly, her gaze unfocused. "I... I"

"Did you blow a fuse, little carrot?" I chuckle. "What's your name?"

"Jewel," she replies, confused.

"Seems I haven't come through on any of my promises. That settles it. When a pocket rocket won't do, you need to whip out the purple-headed love warrior."

I pick her up, her legs wrapped around my waist, pussy still clenched around my beaded cock. Pulling out of her conduit, I toss her onto the bed. Her eyes widen as I rotate cocks in front of her, trying to find my pièce de résistance. I flash her a wicked grin when I finally find it. Or should I say, them? The top cock is thick and ridged, perfect for grinding with a knob designed to hit the g-spot perfectly. The smaller dick beneath is longer and slimmer, curving out before narrowing to a soft point at the end. Small bumps cover the edges, giving it a texture I know she'll enjoy.

She swallows and then licks her lips, her eyes locked on my throbbing thrill hammer.

"Like what you see?"

I give the boys a stroke, slicking them up. Crawling on top of her body, I move like an apex predator, not the primary consumer I am. Rubbing my cock along her wet pussy, I lean down to whisper in her ear, "It's going to feel so good when I stuff your anode with my cathode."

A gasp leaves her lips even as she looks at me with confusion. I suppose my dirty talk is a little unusual compared to what she's experienced. Undeterred, I continue rubbing my cock against her pussy, letting her feel every ridge as I rub my paw against her tight hole.

"I'm going to overload you until you short circuit."

She starts trembling beneath me, already hypersensitive. "Wattson," she moans.

"Yes, little carrot?"

"Please, I," she breaks off into another moan as I press harder into her clit with each thrust. I could tease her all night. We've barely dipped into my power stores, but my sweet carrot decides she's done with the teasing and grabs ahold of my ears.

"Volta!" I cry out. It's her turn to laugh now.

"Two can play this game!" She gives each ear a firm stroke. "Now complete this circuit, bunny, or I'll go back to lone rangering."

"I'd hate for you to have to issue a customer complaint," I say as I slowly push into her. Her pussy is wet and ready for me, but

I want to work into her ass slowly. As my bottom cock pushes past the tight ring of muscle, my Jewel lets out a moan.

"That's it, little carrot. I'm going to fill you up until you're bursting. My electric love juice will power you for days." Her grip tightens, the circulation to my ears being temporarily cut off.

"Fuck!" She releases her grip when I shout.

"Too much?" She looks at me with concern in her eyes.

"No, little carrot. It hertz so good." Nibbling her neck, my ears fall back in her face. A current shoots through me when she licks one of my ears as I bottom out. Slowly, I pull back nearly to the tips of my cocks before thrusting into her, hard. A deep moan escapes me as she responds with a tug of one ear and a bite of the other. Turns out my little carrot is a bit spicy.

We continue our battle. Me pounding her hard while she pulls and nibbles at my ears. She gives me a saucy look before rolling me over, taking her turn to run this ride. She has to release my ears, but it's worth it for the view. Though I grab her hips, I let her take control. Sparks fly as she bucks and writhes on my double dongs until her transformer blows.

"Fuck, Wattson!" She starts to slow down as the orgasm courses through her body. But if she's still speaking, it's not enough.

"Keep going, little carrot. You're not at capacity yet. I know you can handle this load."

She keeps riding, head thrown back, chanting garbled nonsense. My paws land on her hips, helping her to hit all the right angles. Her fists clench in my fur moments before her pussy clenches around my cock. Jumbled noises rip from her throat as I fill her with my juice, thrusting a few times to give her every last drop of energy I have. She collapses on top of me, continuing to mumble nonsense.

Once I come down from the overpowering experience, I roll her onto her side, covering her with a fuzzy blanket I find. It's not as soft as my fur, but it'll do for now. Her eyes close as a dreamy smile spreads across her face.

Stroking her hair, I'm reluctant to say goodbye. "Good night, little carrot. I think it's time for me to power down now."

My Jewel snuggles down into her blankets, totally satiated.

"Okay, funny bunny." She murmurs, as she falls over the abyss into a deep sleep.

Chapter 7

Yes, I've Tried Rubbin' My Nubbin

Jewel

My head and my pussy are pounding. What the hell? You know what, maybe this is a sign I should snuggle back down and sleep in while I have the house to myself. God knows what time it is, but honestly, it doesn't matter. I could sleep for three days straight and still be tired.

Rolling onto my back and flipping the blanket over my face to block the light streaming through the window only works for so long. Then the memories from last night slam into my mind.

"Fuck!" Sleep forgotten, I shoot up to sit in the bed, frantically looking around the room. "Wattson?"

No answer.

Did I hallucinate the large pink rabbit that gave me the best multiple orgasms of my life? It was just wine, not edibles or something. I haven't done those since college. The throbbing soreness in my pussy and ass tells me that *something* happened last night, and I don't think I could have done all that with my Jackrabbit 5000 in its normal form.

No, all the evidence, little as it may be, points to Wattson being real. If that's true, where the hell is he? Maybe he's in the kitchen making breakfast. He seems like the kind of man... uh rabbit... who would do that sort of thing.

Groaning, I shove the blanket off me completely so I can swing my legs to get up. The cold of the wood floor seeps into my toes, causing me to shiver. Though, honestly, it could be the fact that I'm naked as the day I was born that's making me shiver, not just the temperature of my house.

Padding into the kitchen expecting to see my love bunny, disappointment grips me upon finding it empty. Confused, I wander back towards the bedroom to the en suite bathroom, but he isn't in there either. It's when I turn around to leave the bathroom that I see it.

On the floor by the foot of my bed, my hot pink Jackrabbit 5000 lies lifeless. An inexplicable pang of sadness washes over me before I mentally slap myself.

"So what if he was real, Jewel? Who cares if he gave you the best orgasms of your life?" I lie to myself. "It's not like you could have a giant pink Ohm-azing bunny around, even if he folded your laundry and took care of you for once. Ugh!"

Stomping over to my bed, I stoop down and swipe the toy from the ground. Flicking the switch on causes the whole thing to vibrate wildly, the head of the shaft spinning around and around aimlessly in the air. Telling myself I'm not disappointed that Wattson didn't reappear, I head to the bathroom to give the toy a very thorough cleaning.

Once it's dry and stowed safely away in the back of my night-stand drawer, I resign myself to the fact that mama's playtime is over. No more wild pink hares or screaming orgasms. Instead, they will soon be replaced with my three kiddos and migraines from a different kind of screaming.

It is what it is, I guess, right?

Four days. Four days is all I last without craving Wattson's touch again. Last night, I tried using my Jackrabbit 5000, but I just couldn't make myself come. I mean, I tried *everything*. Watching some porn, adding an extra clit sucker, fantasizing about my night with Wattson... nothing worked. Now I'm frustrated as hell.

I took today off work because I think I will punch the next person who asks me a stupid question, and I really don't need to have an HR nightmare on my hands. Instead, I decided to play hooky and get lunch with my friend Allison, which has turned into more of a boozy brunch than anything else.

"God, you seem so tense, Ruby!" Allison thinks it's funny to call me by a different gemstone each time instead of my name. She's one of my best friends, so she's the only one who could get away with it.

"Yeah, well. You know how it is, Ally." I grumble as I sip on my mimosa.

"Okayyyy, but there's gotta be something you can do! Maybe you need to get laid."

I nearly choke on my drink because I haven't told Allison about Wattson. She wouldn't believe me if I did, so why bother?

"I think I'm good on that front, Ally. How do you expect me to go on a date anyway while I have the kids at home?"

Allison looks thoughtful as she considers my words. If I know her, she's thinking of alternate solutions for my plight.

"Well, ok, but what about a little, ya know, *alone time*." She waggles her eyebrows to emphasize her point. When I don't respond, she must think I don't get her meaning because she continues.

"Ya know... some time tickling your taco. Surfin' the slit. A little Clitty Clity Bang Bang." She emphasizes that last one with finger guns.

"Ally, for the love of all that is holy, please stop. I knew what you meant the first time." I grab her fingers and pull them down to the table, disarming her of her deadly digits. She's going to keep going if I don't shut her up. "Fine, yes, I'll try that. Maybe I'll treat myself to a new battery operated boyfriend while I'm at it."

Seemingly appeased, Allison settles back from the table and happily sips on her drink. Even though she is a little crude about it, she's right in a way. Maybe if I use the Jackrabbit 5000 again, Wattson will come back. It worked last time.

Chapter 8

My Little Carrot

Wattson

Four days. It's been four days since I left Jewel–I mean Case 3247Q–and I can't get her out of my mind. I've never been this obsessed with a case before. Normally I hop out, satisfy the customer, and hop back to headquarters, eager to begin the next case. Not with her.

She consumes my thoughts. Every time I nibble a carrot, I think of her. *My little carrot.* Shaking my head, I resume filling out Form TPS69.

"Procedures, procedures, procedures," I mumble under my breath.

"Wattson, are we experiencing an outage in this vicinity?" The stern voice startles me as my boss hops up behind me.

"You still haven't turned in your report on Case 3247Q. It's overdue. That's not like you, Wattson."

My ears droop when I take in his disappointed stare. "Yes Mr. Farraday, It'll be done in a microsecond, sir."

Mr. Farraday harrumphs and hops away as I hear a cackle from my desk neighbor, Sparky.

"Still hung up on that case, Wattsy-boy? You know you'll retire before those batteries die. Ohm-azing outlasts everyone." His laughter grinds into me as he turns back to his paperwork.

He's right. I know he's right, but a bunny can dream, can't he? And boy, have I been dreaming. Dreaming of the curve of her hips, the swell of her breasts, the taste of her pussy. I need to focus before I have a sudden discharge at work.

Customer left unsatisfied by an inferior competing product. Ohm-azing batteries customer service agent dispatched to rectify situation. Customer resistant to acknowledge superiority of Ohm-azing product, agent proceeded to thoroughly demonstrate usefulness by completing various common household tasks, including: folding and organization of laundry, cunnilingus, and multiple bouts of fornication resulting in no less than four climaxes. Customer expressed full satisfaction and satisfaction agent was recalled to headquarters.

A deep sigh escapes me as I finish up the report. This form does nothing to express how good it felt to be inside her. How her eyes lit up when she first saw my dicks change in front of her. Hearing her scream my name.

Fuck. I want to get back to her. I *need* to get back to her. If only there was a way.

Chapter 9

That's the Correct Use For Tupperware Right?

Jewel

After lunch with Allison, I came straight home to test my theory. The kids won't be home from school for another three hours, so if I want to get some self-love in, now is the time. It's two pm here, but it's five o'clock somewhere, so I pour myself a hefty glass of wine and head into my bedroom.

Why do I feel awkward all of a sudden? Oh, right. Because I'm trying to fuck myself hard enough that a giant pink rabbit with a rotating selection of dildo-cocks apparates in my bedroom. That tracks.

Without bothering to slip out of my sundress–I mean they are made for easy access after all–I lay back on the bed and slip off my panties. Reaching over to grab my trusty drawer dick, a shiver of anticipation runs down my spine. Clicking it on, I get to work.

The first buzz of the toy over my clit already has me panting. Working it lightly up and down over my folds to tease myself is torture. Unable to wait much longer, I press the tip of the vibrator to my sensitive butter bean harder, until I am close to coming. Just before reaching the precipice, I drag the toy back down to my entrance to find I'm dripping wet. Perfect.

Just the tip pressing inside my sopping wet burrow feels exquisite. By the time I get the entire shaft in, I'm near bursting. It doesn't take long before I'm clenching around the toy, my body riding out an explosive orgasm.

The toy is still buzzing inside me when I open my eyes to glance around the room, but my bouncy lover is nowhere to be found. Turning the toy off, I slide it out of me in confusion.

"Shit. What did I do last time?" Thinking back to last weekend, I try to remember what caused Wattson to show up in the first place. Finally, it dawns on me– the batteries died and I replaced them!

Frustration grips me when I realize I just replaced these mere days ago. Ohm-azing batteries last nearly forever. How can I wear them out? Maybe if I just leave it on all day, it will drain the batteries.

Decided, I head to my en suite and turn the toy on its highest setting before setting it on the bathroom counter. The Jackrabbit 5000 sure is hoppin' as it wiggles around and around in circles spurred on by the intense vibrations.

Just as I exit the bathroom, however, a crash has me whipping back around, only to see my poor little buzzy bunny on the floor. The battery compartment lid popped off and two of the batteries fell out, causing my Jackrabbit to hop no more.

"Ugh, that won't work." Grumbling to myself, I head to the kitchen and grab a large tupperware. If I trap the toy in the container, then weigh the container down, it should be safe, right? It's worth a shot, so I head back to my bathroom to set it up.

Ok. Shove the batteries back in, close the compartment lid, flip it on high, drop the vibrator into the tupperware, and seal. Lastly, I put my hair dryer on top of the container to make sure it doesn't move. There. That should do it.

I watch my buzzy buddy flail and thrash in its plastic prison, but it never falls off the counter again. Satisfied, I head to the kitchen to get the dishes done while I wait for the batteries to fade.

After only an hour, my pussy plunger has plunged to an early death. Initially, I'm surprised and a little disappointed because Ohm-azing batteries should last longer than that. Then I remember I stole these from the remotes and kids' toys in a fit of desperation, so of course they were already mostly used.

Giddy, I free my love stick from its enclosure. Replacing the batteries with four fresh ones, I take a deep breath and turn it on. Sure enough, the thing starts going wild, rapidly spinning and vibrating out of control. Placing it on the ground before I step back, I watch as the faint glow reappears around the out-of-control toy.

It's working! God, I hope it's Wattson that this sucker turns into and isn't some, like, randomly assigned Customer Satisfaction Rabbit from Ohm-azing.

With hope in my heart, I call out to the beautiful pink bunny that has appeared in front of me. "Wattson?"

Chapter 10

I Never Back Down From a Challenge

Wattson

"Wattson?" She repeats herself, searching my face for recognition.

Hearing her say my name causes me to pop my breaker. I blink. And blink again. There's no fucking way this is happening. There I was, filling out yet another TPS69 report. This time, I helped out some teens after replacing the dead batteries on their video game controllers. I'm pretty good at eSports, and usually I enjoy mashing buttons and twiddling sticks as much as the next bunny, but somehow all I could think of was Jewel, completely distracting me and ruining my K/D ratio. It's probably too much detail for the report though, and I'm starting a rewrite when suddenly, POW. I'm right back here, with her!

Words dissipate from my mind like degrees from a heat-sink. I can't think of a single thing to say–which never happens. My ears twitch and I blink again, but I'm unable to respond, glitching hard.

I'm standing in front of my little carrot. *My perfect little carrot.* This shouldn't be possible. Her Ohm-azing batteries should've lasted much longer than this; they're the best!

I've probably been bugging out here for 45 seconds, clearly an abnormal amount of time to just stare at someone, when I finally shake my head clear. What does it matter how I got here? I'm here. With her. It's a dream come true.

"Shit. You look exactly like him." She drops her head in her hands, letting out a hysterical laugh. "Look at me. I'm about to cry because my vibrator didn't turn into a specific pink bunny."

She waves a hand in my direction without looking back up. "I'm as satisfied as I can possibly be without Wattson. You can go."

The words warm my heart. My sweet Jewel has been missing me as much as I've been missing her. A smile spreads across my face. Unwilling to watch her despair, I hop over and grab her hands, pulling them away from her face so she can look at me.

"Little carrot, it's me."

She looks at me with watery eyes. "It worked?" She whispers, still not believing what is right in front of her.

My paw shakes as I brush away a single tear that's streaking her cheek. A giggle bursts free before she breaks out into full laughter, more tears than I can catch now streaming down her face. She grabs my face, pulling me close to plant kisses on my forehead, cheek, and neck.

"I didn't know if that would work."

She continues kissing me, murmuring against my fur as she does.

"I can't believe it worked. God Wattson, I've never felt this way about anyone. I can't stop thinking about you. I need you like a circuit needs a load."

Amused at her electric declaration, I kiss her forehead. "I'm so happy to hear that, little carrot. I feel the same way." She kisses my neck and strokes my ears. "What? No laundry this time?" I moan into her touch.

She giggles as she continues stroking me. She's overcharging my capacitor and I'm going to overheat. Pulling back a little, I run my furry thumb over her cheek. "Slow down, little carrot. We've got plenty of time."

And I have so many plans for how to use it.

She grimaces. "Not really. I only have until five before the kids are back. That only gives us…"

I cut her off. "A challenge. While I'd much rather take my time exploring every micron of your body, instead we'll see how many times I can blow your fuse before they get home. We'll turn all this potential energy into kinetic energy."

Backing her up against the wall and pinning her arms above her head, I growl. "Be a good girl and don't move."

Hungry for her, I nibble at her neck as I rotate through my cocks, searching for the one I want. When I find it, I kick open her legs and press my lightning rod right where she needs it. This model doesn't look like much, but it packs a lot of power. With its thick, pulsating head, this spicy eggplant should work perfectly. Vibrations shake her mound, slowly building up the speed. Jewel bites her lip, attempting to follow instructions.

"Does your sweet cunt want more?"

"Please, Wattson."

"Take what you need, little carrot."

She immediately bears down on my stiff cock, wetness from her bare pussy soaking my fur. Closing her eyes, she rests her head back against the wall, completely focused on taking her own pleasure.

"That's it, my Jewel. Do you have any idea how many times I've dreamt about doing this since last weekend? How many times I've thought about touching you, tasting you, *fucking you?*" She lets out a breathy moan. "Are you going to come for me, little carrot?"

"Wattson!" she screams, back arching, legs trembling.

Chuckling, I pull away from her and spin her to face the wall. "And I haven't even gotten you naked yet."

Chapter 11
Is It Waterproof?
Jewel

A paw between my shoulder blades is all it takes for me to lean forward and brace my hands on the wall.

"Mmmm, so eager." Wattson's purr tickles the hairs on the back of my neck. Hell yeah, I'm eager. Anyone would be. Except everyone else is gonna have to get their own Ohm-azing bunny because this one is *mine*.

Wattson pulls back his hips, leaving me momentarily bereft, but then his paws are gliding around my waist to the hem of my dress. That soft, pink fur is feather-soft and heat immediately starts building in my core again. It's like my pussy knows what's coming and is gearing up for a showdown.

Except, that horny bitch doesn't actually know what's coming, does she? *Well, besides me, obviously.* The thought brings a lazy smile to my lips. But the soft whirr of Wattson's multi-cock rotating reminds me–and my eager kitty– that we haven't experienced everything he has to offer. Facing the wall means I can't even see which fun stick he chooses, ratcheting up the excitement and anticipation coursing through my body.

A click resounds in the room, and then Wattson is flipping the skirt of my dress over my hips. Pinned against the wall with my dress in his paws, I'm trapped and at his glorious mercy.

"I can't wait any longer, Jewel. I need to be inside you. Now." His voice is desperate, so intense.

Eagerly, I tilt my hips to push my ass out, giving Wattson the access he needs to shove in whatever tool he's chosen to rearrange my guts with. As he notches against my entrance, his fuckstick starts vibrating wildly.

"Are you ready, little carrot?" A nod and a whimper are all I can manage. "Then brace yourself on the wall, baby, because this is about to be a high rate discharge."

That's all the warning I get before he buries himself to the hilt in one brutal thrust. A scream tears itself from my throat in sync with Wattson's guttural moan as he leans his head against my shoulder.

When he doesn't move right away, I start to squirm against him. That's all it takes for him to rear back and start pounding into me like he's trying to overload an entire city electric grid. The intensity has me collapsing forward, my forehead resting against the rough wall of my bedroom.

Wattson tangles his paw in my hair and unceremoniously yanks it back, forcing my head back and my tits out. The resulting arch in my back allows him to drive even deeper. I never understood the appeal of a dick hitting your cervix until now, but the bite of pain along with the vibrating pleasure sends me over the edge quickly. Wattson doesn't stop though.

"One more, little carrot. Give. Me. One. More." Each word accompanies a hard thrust that has me rolling into my next climax before I can even come down from the last. My cream canal puts a death grip on his clam hammer so tight he's struggling to push into me. That is, until he digs his huge paws into my hips and pulls me back onto his cock with the force of a lightning strike.

With a cry, Wattson fills my spasm chasm with his hot electric essence. The jizz jolt amps me up to my own mind-blowing finish, my juice box squirting lady liquid, drenching both of us.

A brief thought crosses my mind. *Is the fluid bad for my love bunny's electric parts? What if I cause him to short circuit?!"*

Wattson's laugh is stuttered as he pants behind me, but he manages to eke out, "Don't worry, little carrot. You definitely made me short circuit, but all my joysticks are just fine."

"I said my inside thoughts out loud again, didn't I?" Wattson pulls out of me and gently turns me around to face him. Any embarrassment is wiped away by the love radiating back at me in his eyes.

"Funny Bunny, are you here to stay?" My voice is small, concern that he will disappear again evident. Wattson grips either side of my face with those soft paws I love so much before answering.

"I think so, little carrot. The executives at Ohm-azing must have realized that you won't be 100% satisfied without me by your side. Never has an Ohm-azing representative been sent back out to the same client, and I don't feel the familiar pull of the portal that usually zaps me back to headquarters once my job is complete." He pauses to give me a deep kiss, then continues.

"But I promise you this, my priceless Jewel. I want nothing more than to remain here with you, to live life with you. *Nothing*, not even the bigwigs at HQ, is going to get in my way." Wattson's emotional expression turns into a smug grin.

"Besides, this bunny promised you he could keep going and going and going. And I plan to keep that promise for the rest of our lives."

Tears slide down my cheeks because deep down, I know he is telling me the truth. Never did I think I would find true love from buffin' my own muffin, but I won't squander this chance. Wattson is mine, and I'm his. Furever.

Chapter 12
Epilogue
Wattson

My paws stroke the hard length. The hickory is cool to the touch. I feel the comfortable weight against my shoulders and chest. I resist the urge to thrust into it. For now.

I open my eyes and appreciate my new equipment. My new drum weighs heavy on my shoulders. My mallets have a long shaft. Just how I like them. These thicker sticks not only produce more power, but they last longer, too. Just like me. Durability is important when you plan on lasting all night. While I usually prefer a good rubber head, I opted for fleece this time. The thought of Jewel playing with my stick sends a jolt down my spine.

"Mr. Bunny?" The tiny voice pulls me out of my fantasy. I look down to see the oldest of Jewel's kits look up to me with big eyes. "You sure she's going to be OK with this? Seems loud and mom's always telling us to be quiet."

As if responding to their question, the youngest crashes their cymbal. Perhaps a triangle would have been more appropriate for a toddler, but if you're going for volume, nothing beats a three-year-old with a cymbal.

The middle kit cracks a laugh, banging their sticks against their snare drum. Their form is abysmal, but the rhythm isn't bad.

The oldest gives me a worried look.

"It'll be great! Trust me."

As I'm about to second guess my decision, we hear the door open. "Hey everyone, I'm home!" Jewel shuts the door behind her and makes her way into the living room, where we're all waiting for her with wide smiles. She sees us, face paling as she drops her bag onto the ground. With a forced smile, she asks, "Wattson, what exactly is going on here?"

The kids break out into the drum cadence we've been working on since she left for her spa day. Any hint of relaxation she may have attained at the spa is being visibly wiped away as she listens to her children lose track of the beat and fall into their own chaotic, discordant rhythms. She shoots me a death glare.

"Why don't you continue practicing in the garage like we talked about?" Jewel's kits are beaming with pride, despite the questionable performance.

The oldest shuffles up to Jewel. "Did you like it, mom?"

She looks down at them with a smile. "Of course! It was great. Now go practice while I talk with Mr. Wattson."

The kids file out into the garage, shut the door, and continue with their clamor.

"Wattson," she starts.

"Little carrot, it has been far too long since I've heard you scream my name. I promise the kids won't be able to hear a thing while they're practicing. This drum isn't the only thing I want to be banging today." I rub the fleece head up one of her arms. "C'mon, little carrot. Let's go boom boom boom up to our room and make some music of our own."

About Unfortunate Reads

 Cassie is an ADHD millennial mom of one from Baltimore who loves craft beer and chaos. Though she runs the Unfortunate Reads page, she reads and enjoys more than just the absolutely unhinged stories. She likes her books extra spicy, with a special fondness for PNR, Sci/fi, and Why Choose romance.

Cassie is a sex positive, feminist, LGBTQIA+ ally who supports indie authors and human artists. She loves to interact with the bookstagram/booktok communities. There is no room for disparagement of books, authors, or readers on her pages. **Reading is reading!**

She began publishing in 2024, and quickly caught the writing bug. She is also a narrator and generally can't pick one facet of the book world to stay in, which is how she started running the Monsterotica Book Con.

You can find her online at:
Instagram: @unfortunate.reads
TikTok: @unfortunatereads
unfortunatereads.com

Cassie's Other Works

<u>Writing:</u>

The Time of Her Life

Handle Me

Pushin' Cushions (cowritten with Vera Valentine)

<u>Narration:</u>

As Unfortunate Reads:

Stiff by Thea Masen, (Duet narration with Richard Pendragon)

As Aspen Destrier:

The Fire Goddess by Amber Collins

Whatever Works by Amber Collins

The Shrinking App by Amber Collins

The Wellington Ruse by Sarah Welk Baynum

About Nicole Parker

Nicole Parker is an AuDHD, 30-something California native who spends the great majority of her free time writing books, reading books, or organizing her ever growing TBR list. She also has a spouse, some kids, and pets, but this isn't about them.

She began publishing in 2024 after quickly falling in love with the sentient object romance world. She took the concept of "there are no bad ideas" to heart and really ran with it.

Nicole's Other Works

BONUS IF YOU'VE MADE IT THIS FAR...

This was legitimately the mockup I gave the talented Kit Fox Art when I commissioned her. She magically turned it into the cover you see on this book.

Thank your artists, y'all. Especially the ones who don't blink when you ask them to draw a giant pink bunny with rotating cocks.